COVER

In 1996, a volume was published, celebrating sixty years of The Broons and Oor Wullie. Now as the stories' seventieth anniversary approaches, we present the tenth book in the series.

The stories were originally brought to life by the inspiration of Robert D. Low, the Managing Editor, and legendary illustrator Dudley D. Watkins. The great majority of strips in this retrospective will feature Dudley Watkins' artwork, but also highlighted will be a few pages by some of his illustrious successors, such as Ken Harrison and current artist, Peter Davidson.

We present the covers of these volumes, which have proved hugely popular over the past ten years.

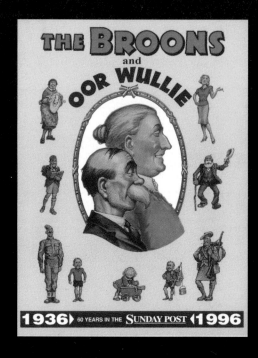

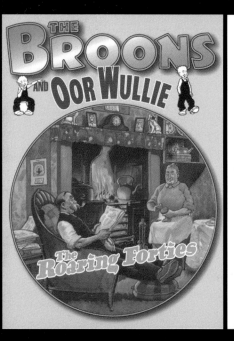

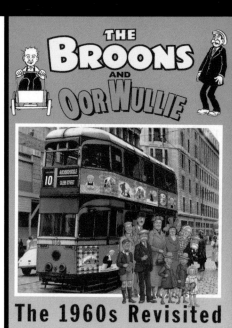

STORY

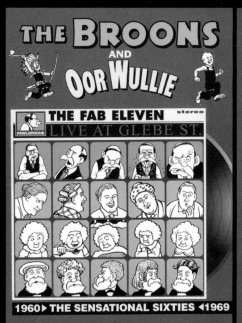

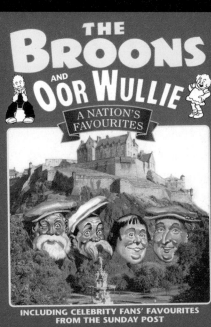

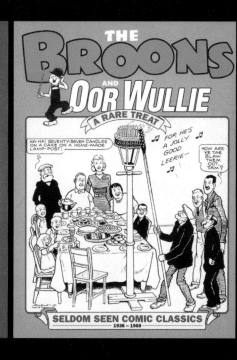

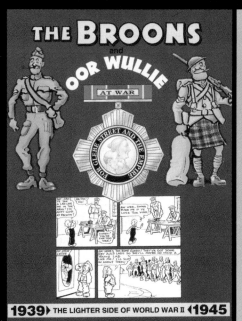

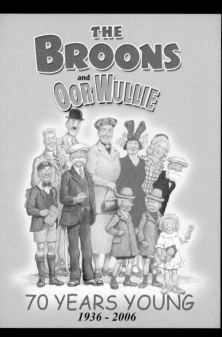

1936

THE SUNDAY POST, DECEMBER 13, 19 36.

The Sunday Post

NO. 1633. [REGISTERED AT THE GENERAL POST OFFICE AS A NEWSPAPER.]

PRINTED AND PUBLISHED IN GLASGOW EVERY SUNDAY MORNING.

SUNDAY, DECEMBER 13, 1936.

RICE TWOPENCE.

PROCLAMATION SCENES

People's Welcome To King George VI.

KING GEORGE VI. YESTERDAY AFTERNOON DROVE TO BUCKINGHAM PALACE, AND THEN TO ST JAMES'S PALACE, WHERE HE TOOK THE OATH OF ACCESSION BEFORE A SPECIAL SESSION OF THE PRIVY COUNCIL.

DECEMBER 13, 1936

In the year The Broons and Oor Wullie first appeared, a constitutional crisis rocked the country. King Edward the eighth had abdicated, and King George the sixth came to the throne. The Sunday Post of December the thirteenth dedicated the entire front page to the news.

THEIR MAJESTIES OF SCOTLAND

Bound are we to his Throne by chains ;
The chains of ancient vows,
The undimmed kingship of his Sire,
The virtue of his House,
His own escutcheon proved in War
And proved in Peace again,
His clear concept of Monarchy,
His walk with common men.

Enough to hold this land to him,
Our Man before the world
Keeping our steady pride of place
— The rest in faction h...
Enough !...

The Sunday Post 16th August 1936

The Sunday Post 27th September 1936

The Sunday Post 21st February 1937

The Sunday Post 5th December 1937

The Sunday Post 12th December 1937

The Sunday Post 9th January 1938

The Sunday Post 7th August 1938

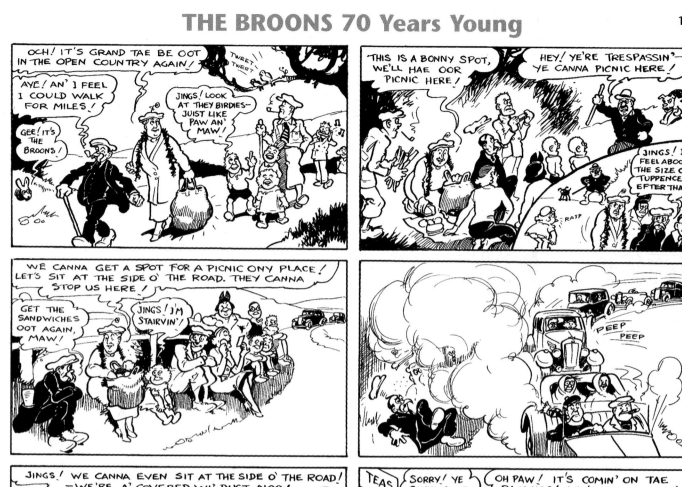

The Sunday Post 17th April 1938

ALWAYS REMEMBER BOYS, THAT "HONESTY IS THE BEST POLICY". NEVER SAY YOU'LL DO A THING AND NOT MEAN IT!

I'M GOIN' TAE TURN OVER A NEW LEAF AN' BE HONEST AN' NEVER STEAL ONY-THING!

MAW! I'M GOIN' TAE BE A DIFFERENT WULLIE! I'LL NEVER TAK ONYTHING IF YE SAY I'M NO' TO!

THAT'S A GUID LADDIE! I CAN TRUST YE THEN TAE STICK IN TAE YER HOME LESSONS WHEN I'M OOT THE NICHT. I'VE MADE SOME CANDY AN' LOCKED IT IN THE PRESS!

LATER

NOO GET ON WI' YER LESSONS, WULLIE!

AYE! TA-TA! MAW.

NOW, SHOULD I, OR SHOULD I NO,—HAE A LOOK FOR THE KEY TAE OPEN THE PRESS TAE SEE WHIT KIND O' CANDY IT IS!

OCH AYE, I WILL, THEN I'LL START MA HOME LESSONS!

NA! IT'S NO' HERE!

JINGS! THE KEY'S NO IN THE COAL BUNKER! IT'S NO ONLY PLACE!

I'LL TRY TAE FORCE OPEN THE DOOR!

SPLIT! JINGS! MA GUID PEN-KNIFE!

AW! GEE.!! I'LL LOSE MA RAG YET!

I CANNA GET THE KEY O' THAT PRESS AT A'! AN' I COULD HAE BEEN DAEIN' MA HOME WORK A' THIS TIME— I'LL GET A BELTIN' FRAE THE TEACHER THE MORN!

GOSH! HERE'S MAW COMIN' NOW!

HULLO WULLIE, HAE YE BEEN BUSY?

AYE, MAW!

—LOOKIN' FOR SOMETHIN'.?

NOW YOU BRING ME YER SCHOOL BAG—I WANT TAE SEE YER HOME-WORK!

I THINK I KEN WHIT YE'VE BEEN LOOKIN' FOR!

—IT'S THIS,— THE KEY O' THE PRESS.—I KENT YE'D NEVER OPEN YER BAG, SO I HID THE KEY INSIDE!

I NEVER THOCHT THAT MAW WIS AS SMAIRT AS THAT!

The Sunday Post 5th February 1939

The Sunday Post 15th January 1939

OOR WULLIE 70 Years Young

The Sunday Post 2nd April 1939

The Sunday Post 9th June 1940

OOR WULLIE 70 Years Young

The Sunday Post 14th July 1940

The Sunday Post 11th August 1940

OOR WULLIE 70 Years Young

The Sunday Post 25th May 1941

The Sunday Post 28th September 1941

THE BROONS 70 Years Young

The Sunday Post 25th January 1942

The Sunday Post 22nd November 1942

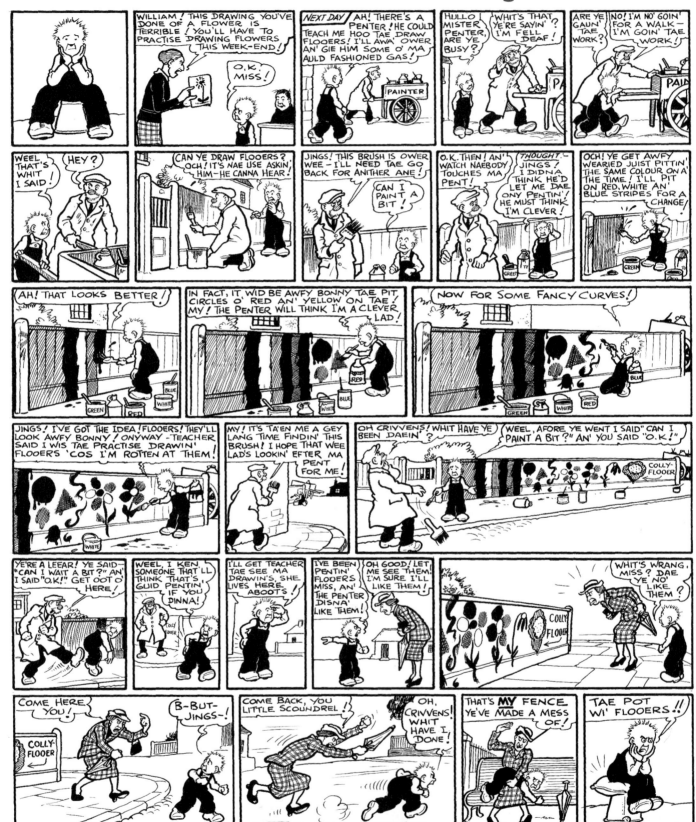

The Sunday Post 14th February 1943

The Sunday Post 8th August 1943

OOR WULLIE 70 Years Young

The Sunday Post 20th June 1943

The Sunday Post 16th January 1944

OOR WULLIE 70 Years Young

The Sunday Post 9th April 1944

The Sunday Post 24th September 1944

The Sunday Post 1st April 1945

The Sunday Post 23rd September 1945

The Sunday Post 3rd June 1945

1946

THE SUNDAY POST, APRIL 14, 1946.

The Sunday Post

No. 2120.

PRINTED AND PUBLISHED IN GLASGOW EVERY SUNDAY MORNING.

[REGISTERED AT THE GENERAL POST OFFICE AS A NEWSPAPER.]

SUNDAY, APRIL 14, 1946.

RADIO—PAGE 13

PRICE TWOPENCE.

Morning Special

A GREAT DAY FOR SCOTLAND

Hampden Howl Rocked Glasgow

AULD ENEMY LAID LOW IN TWO CITIES

At ten minutes to five yesterday afternoon the greatest Hampden howl yet shook Glasgow.

A dramatic last-minute goal had brought Scotland her first soccer triumph over England since 1942.

A few minutes earlier, 60,600 people at Murrayfield, Edinburgh, were shouting enthusiastically for a Scottish rugby team that had swamped England with a record score.

It was a great double for Scotland.

About 200,000 spectators saw the games. 138,000 were at Hampden Park.

That wonderful moment, when the Hampden roar became thunderous, and thousands of hats, jimmies, bonnets, and bottles flew in the air, made up for everything (writes a "Sunday Post" woman in the crowd).

It was worth the long, long trail to Hampden, two hours' wait before the game started, the cramped limbs, the dig in the ribs, squashed corns, and restricted breathing.

A gallant Scots team had beaten England by one goal, one minute before the final whistle, and a grand international crowd took off their hats to them.

They took them off, too, before the start of the game—to fan themselves in a blazing sun above all afternoon. ...ing to the brightness of tartan ros-... thistles, and demob. suits.

Pies From a Pram

Outside a boy sold pies from a pram. Another advertised corned beef sandwiches at three for a shilling. And a ... man asked a policeman on a white horse if he "couldna ha'e got a tartan ...?"

By two o'clock Hampden seemed ...ed. Yet policemen were still direct-...g spectators to their places, and the ...ice from the control box indicated ...here there was still plenty of room.

Soon the fringe of the crowd was ...corated by a colourful array of lem-...ade bottles, and distress hankies ...re waving merrily to cries of "Carry ...the body."

...sic by military and massed pipe ...ds and a grand gymnastic display ...cadets kept the crowd entertained ...il the big moment when they roared ...ir welcome to the teams.

They kept on roaring—for Scotland ...t off to a flying start. All eyes ...re on the four reserves called on to ...place injured Scots.

Pitman Hero

Big boy Brennan was a hero from ...e start. The six-foot-two miner, ...aying in his first 'National', was ...very first to get his head to the ball. ...here were cheers of encouragement. ...he crowd began to heave and ...sway...

Collars and ties were removed. ...dvice to players and referee floated ... the air— "Give it to Willie!" ..."Don't put it there!" "Remember ...golden and gie us a goal!"

body was sunburnt down one side of the face.

Goal!

In the second half all the players seemed to be nursing some sore part or other. Trainers were running round with sponges and the crowd was yellin, "Dinna bother gettin' yer laces washed. Get on wi' the game."

The roar got louder. Waddell hit the bar. Liddell put the rebound over the bar. Groans rose and fell. Compton broke a flag post. Someone stuck it in.

The minutes went by. One to go! And while the roar rose in one thunderous crescendo, Jimmy Delaney scored.

Everything went into the air. People laughed, cried, shook hands.

Yes, it was worth...

Well Beha...

From first to last, ...ments went like clockw...

The good humour of th... was marked from the ti... were opened at 12.30. ... the Glasgow police, it ... behaved crowd at any ...

Not a single arrest was ... 400 policemen on duty.

Casualties among spec... surprisingly few comp... previous games. Fifty-five ... were treated by the 150 St... Ambulance men at the ... were taken to the Victoria ... Two were victims of sudd... one an ankle injury, and an... a facial wound.

Crowds at Waverley Stati... burgh, bound for Hampd... swelled by the big inflow o... enthusiasts.

Between 8.50 and 11 o'cloc... relief trains were added to the ... run for the soccer crowds.

The rugby men besieged ... stance at St Andrews Square ... steady stream of buses left f... west.

Never before at Murrayfield ha... Scots won by so large a margin... England.

HE DANCED A JIG!

When Scotland's goal was scored, a jubilant spectator rushed on to the field to congratulate the players.

Two policemen nabbed him and led him back to his place—but not before he had thrown his hat in the air half a dozen times, and danced a jig with the policeman hanging on to him.

"Near misses" drew groans and moans from thousands of throats.

"Wee Drappies"

Half-time came without a goal. But hope was high in every Scottish heart. Out came the cheese, sandwiches and the "wee drappies." An English-man lent a bottle opener to a Scots-man, who replied with the offer of a biscuit.

Footballers past and present were praised and deplored. Then some-body made the discovery that every-

HOW DO, NELSON!

From out of the Saturday afternoon crowds in Trafalgar Square yesterday a man sauntered up to Nelson's Column, jumped on its base, and climbed the scaffolding laddering to the top of the Column, just below the figure of the hero of Trafalgar.

Then he went on up to Nelson, and perched around for about five minutes.

At 185 feet above London, he was watched by every eye in Trafalgar Square.

He then came down and found a policeman waiting for him.

Jet Plane Men Quit— Raw Deal Alleged

"In the national interest during the war, we have been sucked ... like an oranj..."

...ded that from the moment the Government acquired the com-pany, work on realistic engines ap-peared to have been retarded at the factory.

Staggering!

Fifty million people drink alcoholic liquor in the U.S.A.

Of these, 3,000,000 are excessive drinkers and 750,000 "chronic alcoholics."

The country has 13,500 cases of alcoholic insanity and "alcoholic psychosis."

So says a report by the "Research Council on Problems of Alcohol."

Cost of caring for alcoholics in mental hospitals is £3,250,000, and of maintaining drunken persons in gaol £6,250,000.

STEEL—PEER'S WARNING

Viscount Samuel at Westminster yester-day, declared nationalisation of the iron and steel industry must not be handled in a slap-dash methods. If the...

38

How The Clyde Helped To Win The War

The Sunday Post, April 28, 1946. 13

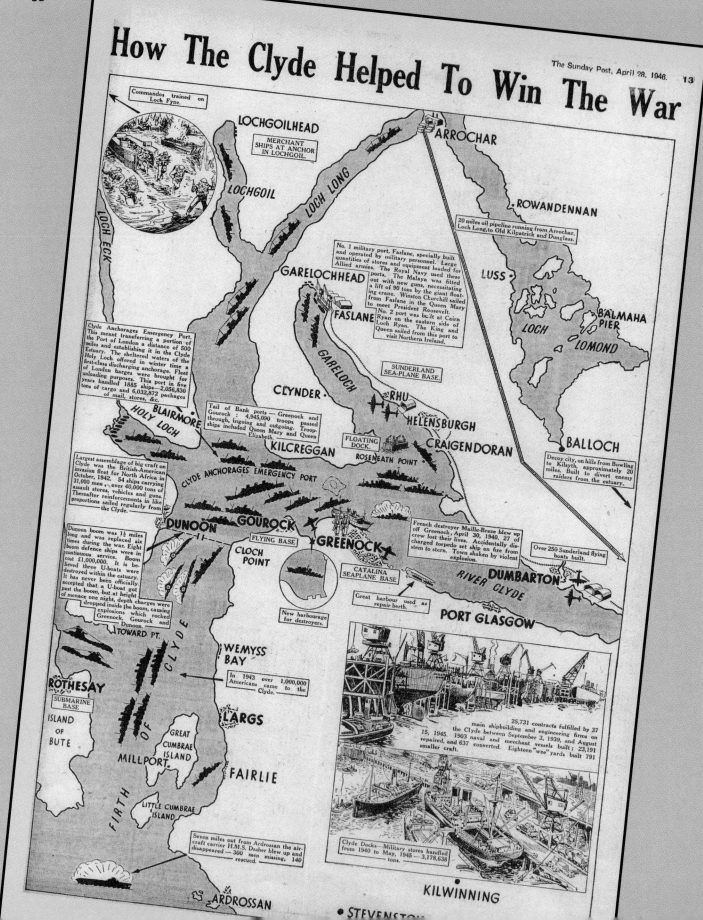

Commandos trained on Loch Fyne.

MERCHANT SHIPS AT ANCHOR IN LOCHGOIL.

LOCHGOILHEAD

ARROCHAR

LOCH GOIL

LOCH LONG

ROWANDENNAN

LOCH ECK

20 miles oil pipeline running from Arrochar, Loch Long, to Old Kilpatrick and Dunglass.

No. 1 military port, Faslane, specially built and operated by military personnel. Large quantities of stores and equipment loaded for Allied armies. The Royal Navy used these ports. The Malaya was fitted out with new guns, necessitating a lift of 90 tons by the giant floating crane. Winston Churchill sailed from Faslane in the Queen Mary to meet President Roosevelt. No. 2 port was built at Cairn Ryan on the eastern side of Loch Ryan. The King and Queen sailed from this port to visit Northern Ireland.

GARELOCHHEAD

LUSS

FASLANE

BALMAHA PIER

LOCH LOMOND

Clyde Anchorages Emergency Port. This meant transferring a portion of the Port of London a distance of 500 miles and establishing it in the Clyde Estuary. The sheltered waters of the Holy Loch offered in winter time a first-class discharging anchorage. Fleet of London barges were brought for unloading purposes. This port in five years handled 1885 ships—2,056,830 tons of cargo and 6,032,872 packages of mail, stores, &c.

SUNDERLAND SEA-PLANE BASE.

GARELOCH

RHU

CLYNDER

HELENSBURGH

BALLOCH

BLAIRMORE

HOLY LOCH

Tail of Bank ports — Greenock and Gourock 4,945,090 troops passed through, ingoing and outgoing. Troopships included Queen Mary and Queen Elizabeth.

FLOATING DOCK.

CRAIGENDORAN

Decoy city, on hills from Bowling to Kilsyth, approximately 20 miles. Built to divert enemy raiders from the estuary.

KILCREGGAN

ROSENEATH POINT

Largest assemblage of big craft on Clyde was the British-American invasion fleet for North Africa in October, 1942. 54 ships carrying 31,000 men—over 40,000 tons of assault stores, vehicles and guns. Thereafter reinforcements in like proportions sailed regularly from the Clyde.

CLYDE ANCHORAGES EMERGENCY PORT

Dunoon boom was 1½ miles long and was replaced six times during the war. Eight boom defence ships were in continuous service. Boom cost £1,000,000. It is believed three U-boats were destroyed within the estuary. It has never been officially accepted that a U-boat got past the boom, but at height of menace one night, depth charges were dropped inside the boom, causing explosions which rocked Greenock, Gourock and Dunoon.

DUNOON

GOUROCK

GREENOCK

FLYING BASE

CLOCH POINT

CATALINA SEAPLANE BASE

French destroyer Maille-Breze blew up off Greenock, April 30, 1940. 27 of crew lost their lives. Accidentally discharged torpedo set ship on fire from stem to stern. Town shaken by violent explosion.

Over 250 Sunderland flying boats built.

RIVER CLYDE

DUMBARTON

New harbourage for destroyers.

Great harbour used as repair berth.

PORT GLASGOW

TOWARD PT.

WEMYSS BAY

In 1943 over 1,000,000 Americans came to the Clyde.

ROTHESAY

SUBMARINE BASE

ISLAND OF BUTE

FIRTH OF CLYDE

LARGS

GREAT CUMBRAE ISLAND

MILLPORT

FAIRLIE

LITTLE CUMBRAE ISLAND

25,731 contracts fulfilled by 37 main shipbuilding and engineering firms on the Clyde between September 3, 1939, and August 15, 1945. 1903 naval and merchant vessels built; 23,191 repaired, and 637 converted. Eighteen "wee" yards built 791 smaller craft.

Seven miles out from Ardrossan the aircraft carrier H.M.S. Dasher blew up and disappeared — 300 men missing, 140 rescued.

Clyde Docks—Military stores handled from 1940 to May, 1945—3,178,638 tons.

KILWINNING

ARDROSSAN

STEVENSTON

The Sunday Post 25th August 1946

OOR WULLIE 70 Years Young

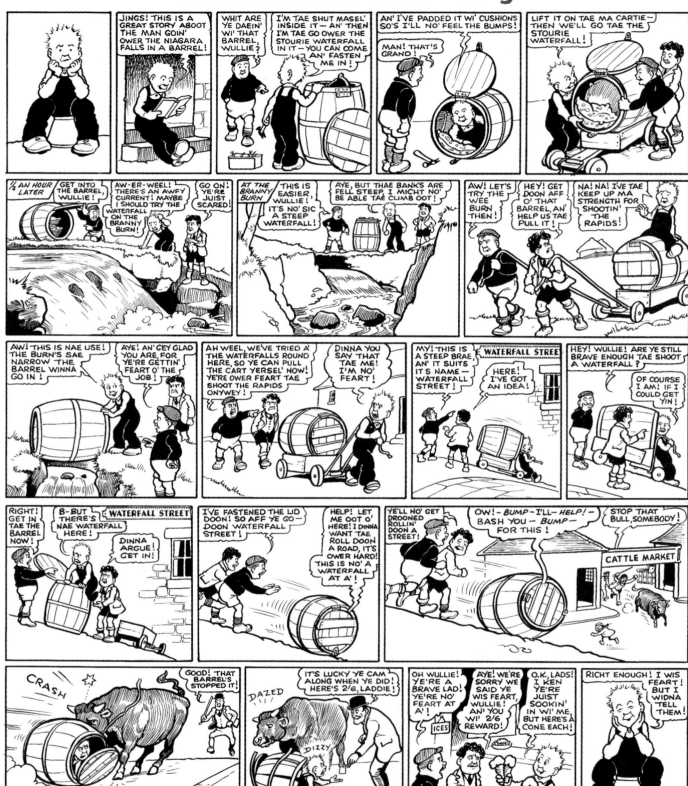

The Sunday Post 3rd November 1946

OOR WULLIE 70 Years Young

The Sunday Post 18th May 1947

The Sunday Post 6th April 1947

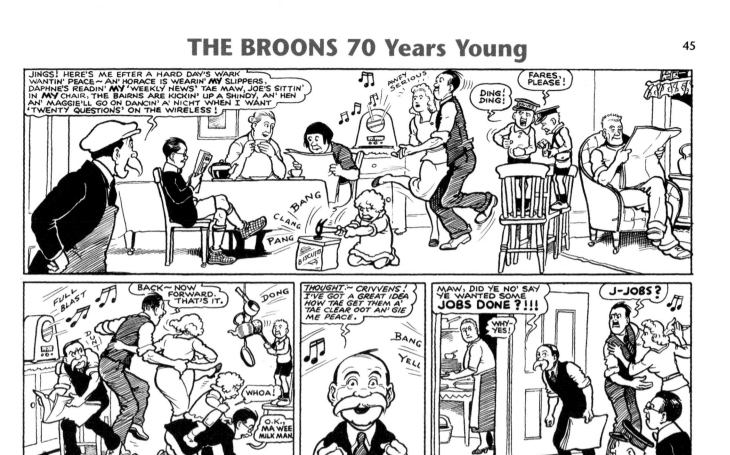

The Sunday Post 4th January 1948

A "don't try this at home" story. Themes such as these would be avoided in the present day.

The Sunday Post 19th December 1948

The Sunday Post 16th May 1948

The Sunday Post 22nd May 1949

The Sunday Post 29th May 1949

The Sunday Post 23rd July 1950

OOR WULLIE 70 Years Young

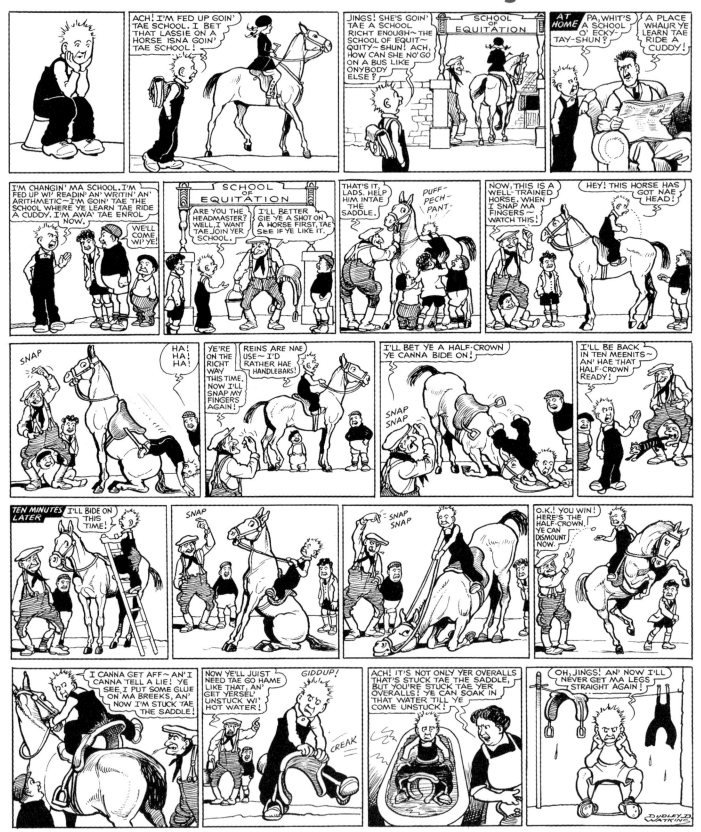

The Sunday Post 16th April 1950

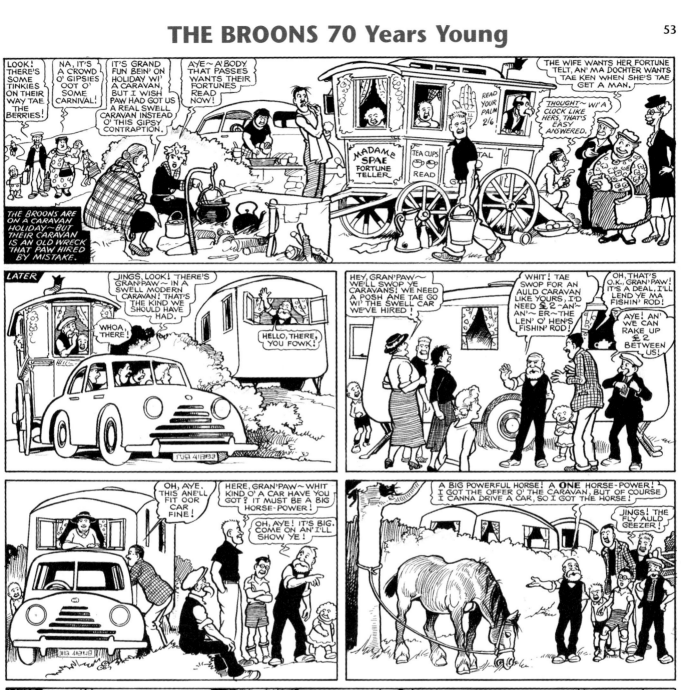

The Sunday Post 30th July 1950

OOR WULLIE 70 Years Young

The Sunday Post 11th February 1951

The Sunday Post 17th February 1952

The Sunday Post 30th March 1952

The Sunday Post 10th August 1952

The Sunday Post 30th August 1953

The Sunday Post 10th January 1954

The Sunday Post 23rd May 1954

The Sunday Post 19th September 1954

OOR WULLIE 70 Years Young

The Sunday Post 22nd May 1955

THE BROONS 70 Years Young

The Sunday Post 20th March 1955

OOR WULLIE 70 Years Young

The Sunday Post 5th June 1955

1956

THE SUNDAY POST, JANUARY 8, 1956.

The Sunday Post

PRINTED AND PUBLISHED EVERY SUNDAY MORNING.

No. 2628

[REGISTERED AT THE GENERAL POST OFFICE AS A NEWSPAPER.]

SUNDAY, JANUARY 8, 1956.

Radio and TV—Page 4.

Morning Special

PRICE 3d

Lucky Black Cat!

U.S. Has "Unbelievably Powerful Weapon"

WORLD'S GREATEST EXPLOSIONS SOON

THE United States will probably explode two hydrogen bombs in a new series of tests in the Pacific early this year, and cause the greatest explosions the world has ever known.

This was announced in Washington yesterday.

The biggest blast will come from a bomb dropped from the air.

In 1952 and in 1954 the U.S. exploded hydrogen bombs in the Eniwetok Islands.

They were so big they had to be housed in sheds, and were far too large to be carried by an aircraft.

But the U.S. has now developed an almost unbelievably powerful weapon, small enough to be delivered by modern atom-bombers, said Congressional sources yesterday.

A Soviet test last November was reported to have been between one to five megatons.

There were reports that the United States planned to detonate an even bigger bomb—perhaps in the order of 30 megatons—immediately after the 1954 blast.

But this plan was shelved temporarily, some sources said, because of the widespread radioactive fall-out from the earlier explosion, which produced protests from abroad.

Japanese fishermen in boats operating outside the officially proclaimed danger area were exposed to radiation.

New explosions will be in the Eniwetok testing area in the Pacific.

Under present plans, more than one island site will be used in order to conduct a quick series of tests.

New Trigger

There has been a big school of thought in Washington that the adverse impact on world opinion would outweigh

*A megaton is the explosive equivalent of 1,000,000 tons of T.N.T.

The wedding took place yesterday at St Mary's Church, Ealing, of 21-year-old actress, Miss Helen Lennox, and producer Bryan Blackburn.

EDEN TO RESIGN RUMOUR DENIED

A SURPRISING rumour gained currency last night that Sir Anthony Eden intends to resign the Premiership in a few months' time, and that he will then be succeeded as Prime Minister by Mr R. A. Butler.

This was categorically denied when I made inquiries at 10 Downing Street, writes a political correspondent.

A Downing Street spokesman said, "This story is false and without any foundation whatever."

Friends of the Prime Minister say that he has been in noticeably vigorous health.

This, indeed, was demonstrated to some extent by the fact that he presided on successive days over Cabinet meetings that lasted two ...

... political career.

"In diplomatic quarters there are increasingly strong rumours that his resignation is to be reckoned with in the coming summer."

... crisis of his ...

ARMED GUARD AT DUNDEE GIRL'S WEDDING

A DUNDEE girl was married in Cyprus yesterday—and there was an armed guard at her wedding.

She is 22-year-old Patricia Jane Halley, a secretary at the political office, Middle East Armed Forces, based on Nicosia.

The bridegroom was 24-year-old Lieut. Robert Forester-Bennett, of No. 45 Royal Marine Commando, who comes from Alverstoke, Hampshire.

The wedding took place at the tiny St Andrew's Chapel in Kyrenia, on the north coast of Cyprus.

Before the ceremony, military police with revolvers and Sten guns searched the church and yard for time bombs.

They mounted an armed guard during the ceremony.

Twenty-four officers from No. 45 Royal Marine Commando put their Sten guns aside for a few hours and made a bridal archway with their swords at the wedding.

Robert and Patricia became engaged on November 26, the night when the state of emergency was proclaimed throughout the island.

They had attended the annual Caledonian Society Ball at a Nicosia luxury hotel, but the dance was broken up when a terrorist bomb exploded on the dance floor, injuring five people.

A champagne reception followed the wedding ceremony yesterday.

The couple will spend their honeymoon at Beirut.

The bride is the elder daughter of Mr and Mrs Frank Halley, formerly of Broadcroft, Farington Terrace, Dundee.

She was at school in North Wales, and later at Cape Town. For a time she was on the staff of a bank in Canada.

She went to Cyprus to visit a cousin last year.

Dies In Vapour Bath

MR JACK STEAN, aged 61, of Handel Way, Edgware, Middlesex, collapsed and died last night while taking a vapour bath at Poplar Baths.

Blizzard Hits North

HEAVY snow fell last night in Aberdeen and many parts of the North-East.

In Aberdeen conditions were particularly bad between 7 p.m. and 8 ...

Blinding snow showers cut visibility in the street ...

traffic had to proceed with great caution.

The melting snow on the road surfaces made conditions trying.

A telephone round-up last night showed that snow ...

Detectives Search Near Murder Tee

POLICE investigations yesterday switched back from Blantyre to East Kilbride, as the hunt for the murderer of 17-year-old Ann Kneilands entered its ...

Armed with stout sticks they probed in deep mud at the end of an unfinished road leading to the ...

6   The Sunday Post, December 30, 1956.

They've Never Had A Hogmanay Like It

Collie Brings 'Em In To Roost!

WHILE visiting a farm last week, I was amazed to see a collie bringing in the turkeys to roost! He divided them into two bunches and drove them into different sheds.

The turkeys didn't seem to mind and the farmer's wife said she couldn't do without him.—Miss Taylor, Fardel Cottage, Glenfarg, Perth.

THE Old Year is almost over and out here in Cyprus we regard the New Year as the one time when we feel really connected with home.

It will be a sad and lonely one for many of us. We have lost friends in the fighting, both in Egypt and Cyprus. We have lost the sweethearts who just couldn't wait for us. And we'll miss the lucky ones who are going home.

But we've arranged a special double celebration. When it is 10 p.m. in Scotland, we'll be toasting the New Year in Cyprus.

And when you lift your glasses at midnight, G.M.T., you'll know that 50 or 60 Jocks, 2000 miles away, will be sending you a silent "Guid New Year tae ane and a'."—J. Rogan, R.A.F., Ayios Nikolas, B.F.P.O. 53, Cyprus.

"If you think eight hours is long enough for a fair trial, Ah'll waken him up."

★ POST BAG

● I notice foreign readers have been sending foreign stamps to someone who now can't accept any more. Perhaps they would like to send them to the Boy Scouts International Bureau, 132 Ebury St., London, which uses them to raise funds.—S. Hunter, 34 Gray St., Kelvingrove, Glasgow.

● Friends warned me, a Londoner, against taking my family to settle down in Glasgow. They said it was a grim, mean city. How wrong they were! I've met nothing but kindness and hospitality from the Scots.—R. Miller, 2b Hollybrook St., Govanhill.

● Last Saturday night my sister arrived seven hours late on the London train. Wouldn't it speed things up if signalmen and train crews had radio sets to keep in touch when there's dense fog?—Janet Scott, 86 Dickson St., Edinburgh.

● I received a Christmas card from Lancashire which had Edinburgh missed out of the address. This is a great credit to the G.P.O., especially at this time.—Mrs Brydon, 185 Broughton Rd., Edinburgh.

● When we unpacked our Christmas tree there was a beautiful bird's nest in the branches! We're leaving it there with little coloured eggs made of sweets.—Sylvia Spreng (aged 12), 70 Inchview Tce., Edinburgh.

● The other day my young son was eating a pomegranate. He shouted, "We're rich!" and produced a pearl from inside it. On examination, I found it was only a bead, but how it got in there beats me!—Mrs Brown, 67 Cumbrae Tce., Kirkcaldy.

● I want the person who stole my childrens' pet rabbit from its hutch on Christmas morning to know he ruined their day. I also hope he got a few bites and scratches.—Mrs Fotheringham, 10 Dalrymple Cres., Musselburgh.

Thoughtful Milk Boy

MY milk boy left this note under the bottle on Christmas morning — "Dear Customer, Thank you very much for the Christmas tip." I would also like to take this opportunity of wishing you and all in your house a very merry Christmas and a happy New Year.

It started our day with a happy feeling. Truly, the younger generation aren't all thoughtless.—Mrs Jeffrey, 75 Greengairs Ave., Glasgow.

It's Words That Count

I READ the letter saying that men always choose Christmas cards without reading the words. I also choose my cards by the lovely pictures.

Recently our minister was in hospital and I selected a lovely "get well" card to send him. I was just about to pay for it, when my young daughter read out the words. "I hope it won't be long till we're together again." After that I've got to be very careful!—Mrs McKenzie, 32 Carfin Street, Govanhill, Glasgow.

On Your Marks!

MY daughter, aged 12, has just been to her first school dance. She told me that, between dances, the boys lined up half-way across the floor and raced for a partner when the music started!

How different from 30 years ago. I can recall a perspiring teacher dragging an embarrassed boy across the hall and thrusting him into my arms.—Mrs Barrie, 1 Kent Dr., Burnside, Rutherglen.

No Justice

I READ your "As We See It" comment about the Briton who had an accident in Belgium and was charged £242 16s for seven weeks in a nursing home.

I went to Canada last year and had to go to hospital—also for seven weeks. I was charged £400 and even had to pay for blood received in a transfusion! You can imagine how I felt on the ship home when I saw several ladies who were going into maternity homes here.—R. MacLean, 68 Glasgow Rd., Kilmarnock.

Well Done, Francis!

I AM looking forward to another year of good reading and enjoyment with the "Sunday Post." And I've a special mention for Francis Gay.

His good deeds are known all over and to the old folk he is a blessing. There would be a lot more lonely and neglected people but for his untiring efforts.—Miss Scott, Briar Cottage, Newstead, Melrose.

Scalp Um Paleface!

I SAW children of all ages with a great array of toys on Christmas morning, but the one who was enjoying himself most was a boy about five years old in full Redskin outfit. He had captured a "paleface"—a wee girl's doll—and was proceeding to scalp it!

I intervened with a few chocolates and the victim was handed back to a wet-eyed owner.—W. Mitchell, 15 Roxburgh St., Edinburgh.

It Was A Risk, But—

IN January of this year, my husband and I and our four children "burnt our boats" in Glasgow and went off to the wilds of Bonnie Strathyre. My husband worked with the Forestry Commission and, for seven months, we revelled in the lovely countryside.

Then we moved to the Carse of Gowrie, where we both work on a farm. I can thresh wheat, pick tatties and shaw neeps—and forget all about city log and climbing stairs. It's been an eventful year.—Mrs McConnell, Glencarse Home Farm, by Perth.

Not So Lucky

MY husband and I are a young couple living in a but and ben. We are determined to better ourselves, so recently my husband gave up a steady job and we sank all our savings in a small van with which he made deliveries to outlying districts.

The venture failed, as we just hadn't the money to last through the petrol rationing. But we're richer in experience and some day we'll try again.—Mrs Mills, 11 Tamworth St., Bridgeton, Glasgow.

By The Vanload!

LAST year I requested readers to send me used Christmas cards for an Orphans' Home. The response was so great that two G.P.O. vans were arriving at my door every day till January 11.

I had to appeal through the B.B.C. to stop sending them. The Orphan Home still has cards to last for many a year and I'd like to assure all these kind people the children are making excellent use of them.—J. Devlin (jnr.), 26 Moss-side Rd., Shawlands, Glasgow.

You'd Never Know Mrs Ramsay Now

IN 1952 I left Kilmarnock for Australia with my wife and two daughters.

What we are most deeply grateful to Australia for is my wife's health. In Scotland she was almost a cripple with arthritis. She improved so much here that she managed to help with the building of our house, and now plays tennis and badminton every week.—R. Ramsay, 3 Bennet Street, Dubbo, N.S.W.

WE'VE been in Australia two years and have quite settled down. We have three daughters—two at school and the other has just left.

We think the education is a lot better here. Children are taught how to conduct themselves with poise in any company, without that paralysing shyness so often found in Britain. There are parents' committees which hold monthly meetings, and the headmaster attends to report on the progress of individual children.—Mrs Muir, 24 Steveys Forest Rd., Oakdale, N.S.W., Australia.

Yearly Mystery

FOR the past four years, on Christmas Day, my boys have received a parcel from a person or persons unknown to me. They would know just how much this means to us, if they could see the joy on my boys' faces as the parcel reveals toys and sweets.

I cannot express how thankful I am.—Mrs Gibson, 23 Lifnock Ave., Hurlford.

Best Policy?

WHILE shopping in a large store the other day, I found a handbag containing 10 £1 notes. I handed it in at the office.

On calling next morning, I found it had been claimed and my reward was 1s 6d! I returned it, wondering if this encourages honesty.—Mrs Blow, 62 Prince St., Peterhead.

* * *

Send your letters to—"Readers' Page, The Sund...

CROSSWORD

ACROSS.
1—He's a relatively monastic type. 4—Mould according to a pattern. 9—Place of entertainment. 10—Comfortable and warm. 11—Part of a fish hook. 12—Mechanical man. 13—Violent attack. 16—Lawful. 18—Time for a bonnet parade! 19—Thrown in athletic contests. 23—Stupid or crowded. 25—Musical play. 27—Swallow greedily. 29—Heath. 30—Expel. 31—A great whirlpool. 32—Small ornament. 33—Natural height.

DOWN.
1—Musical instrument with deep base tone. 2—Disorderly knot of threads. 3—Impatient and keen. 5—Assign. 6—Stumble along painfully. 7—A game. 8—Well-founded. 14—A rustic. 15—Name of distinction. 16—Lariat gives the girl nothing. 17—Used for measuring. 20—Unyielding. 21—Sullen. 22—A diversion is all over to start. 24—Religious discourse. 26—Up to time. 27—Aquatic bird. 28—Small white heron.

Sent in by John H. Gilchrist, 35 Old Lanark Rd., Carluke.

LAST WEEK'S SOLUTION.

Across—1 Cornice, 5 Bolster, 9 Nemesis, 10 Adamant, 11 Operate, 12 Erudite, 15 Red, 15 Fossie, 17 Bright, 18 Negre, 19 Onward, 22 Nasser, 26 Are, 28 Caravan, 29 Natural, 30 Swallow, 31 Imagine, 32 Shelter, 33 Tatters.

Down—1 Consort, 2 Rompers, 3 Install, 4 Exeter, 5 Blamed, 6 Leaguer, 7 Trading, 8 Retreat, 14 Elgar, 16 End, 17 Bos, 19 Oncosts, 20 Warfare, 21 Rivulet, 23 Attract, 24 Survive, 25 Rollers, 26 Answer, 27 Enlist.

The Sunday Post 15th January 1956

OOR WULLIE 70 Years Young

The Sunday Post 22nd July 1956

The Sunday Post 30th September 1956

OOR WULLIE 70 Years Young

The Sunday Post 27th January 1957

The Sunday Post 10th March 1957

OOR WULLIE 70 Years Young

The Sunday Post 23rd November 1958

OOR WULLIE 70 Years Young

The Sunday Post 4th May 1958

THE BROONS 70 Years Young

The Sunday Post 30th November 1958

OOR WULLIE 70 Years Young

The Sunday Post 1st March 1959

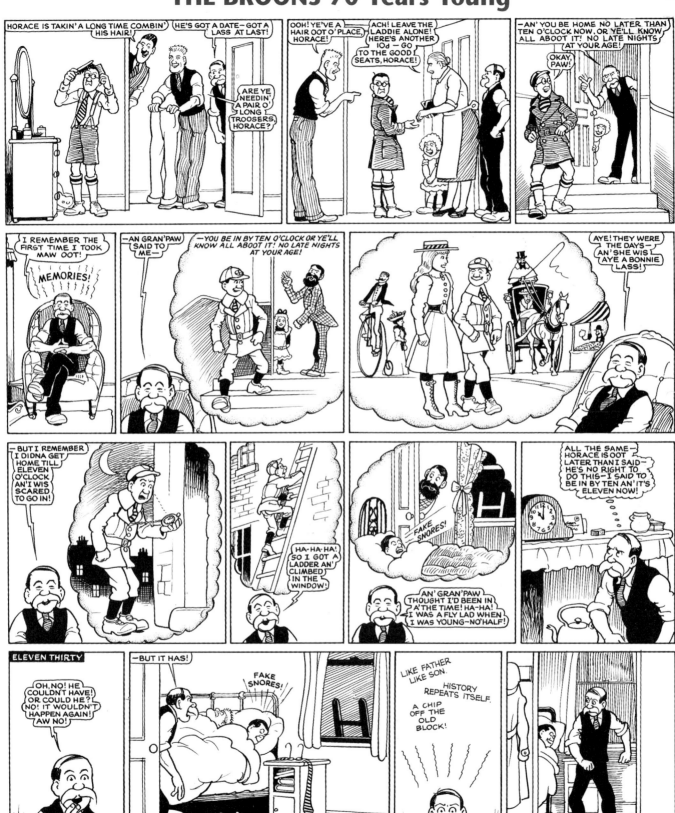

The Sunday Post 8th February 1959

OOR WULLIE 70 Years Young

The Sunday Post 8th March 1959

The Sunday Post 12th June 1960

OOR WULLIE 70 Years Young

The Sunday Post 10th April 1960

THE BROONS 70 Years Young

The Sunday Post 3rd July 1960

OOR WULLIE 70 Years Young

The Sunday Post 1st January 1961

THE BROONS 70 Years Young

The Sunday Post 1st January 1961

The Sunday Post 16th April 1961

The Sunday Post 25th November 1962

OOR WULLIE 70 Years Young

The Sunday Post 21st January 1962

The Sunday Post 2nd December 1962

OOR WULLIE 70 Years Young

The Sunday Post 2nd June 1963

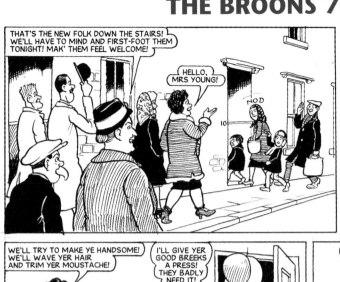

The Sunday Post 29th December 1963

OOR WULLIE 70 Years Young

The Sunday Post 23rd June 1963

THE BROONS 70 Years Young

The Sunday Post 5th January 1964

OOR WULLIE 70 Years Young

The Sunday Post 3rd May 1964

The Sunday Post 23rd February 1964

The Sunday Post 31st January 1965

OOR WULLIE 70 Years Young

The Sunday Post 11th April 1965

1966

The Sunday Post, May 22, 1966.

The Sunday Post

No. 3169

[REGISTERED AT THE GENERAL POST OFFICE AS A NEWSPAPER.]

PRINTED AND PUBLISHED EVERY SUNDAY MORNING.

SUNDAY, MAY 22, 1966.

Morning Special

TV and Radio — Page 26

Price 6d.

CUT LEFT EYE ENDS COOPER'S HOPES

Wife In Tears At Ringside

HISTORY repeated itself at Arsenal football stadium, London, last night when Cassius Clay retained his world heavyweight title by stopping Henry Cooper, of Britain, in the sixth round.

The only difference was that the cut left eye which ruined Cooper's chance of bringing the world heavy-weight title to Britain arrived in the sixth round instead of the fifth.

Otherwise it was all too sadly the same story as at Wembley in 1963. The blood suddenly sprayed from Cooper's eyebrow to signal the end could only be seconds away.

As Cooper was stained red from his face to his waistband, the referee briefly stopped the fight to look at the damage. He waved it on again to give Cooper what could clearly be only a few seconds' grace.

Like a man demented, Cooper hurled himself at the champion. Clay retreated to the ropes. Then he opened up as Cooper, blinded by his own blood, came in head down, hurling both fists at his tormentor.

Another quick look from the referee and the fight was over. As Cooper stamped back to his corner, protesting all the way, the blood spurted out in a thin red arc. His wife, Albina, at the ringside, covered her face in her hands and burst into tears.

Many of those around her must have felt like doing the same. As the fight ended the ring filled, and it was almost 10 minutes before Clay was led away, closely surrounded by policemen.

Great Support

It was a sad but perhaps inevitable end to a heart-warming effort by Cooper, who was supported as he has never been before.

As he came into the ring the Highbury roar must have been heard two miles away and as the National Anthem was played when the gloves were being put on the crowd joined in.

They sang as if to indicate this was their fight as well.

It must have been a highly emotional moment for the British champion Earlier in the day he had said this fight was not just for him but for his country.

● Bill McFarlane's report of the fight is on the back page.

LADY DOROTHY MACMILLAN DIES SUDDENLY

LADY DOROTHY MACMILLAN, wife of the former Prime Minister, Harold Macmillan, died suddenly yesterday at Birch Grove House, Sussex, aged 65.

Lady Dorothy was Dame Grand Cross of the Order of the British Empire.

Earlier this month she was driving her husband on a motor tour of Scotland.

Lady Dorothy met her husband in Ottawa, where her father, the ninth Duke of Devonshire, was Governor - General. The young Harold Macmillan, badly wounded in the First World War, was his A.D.C.

He and Lady Dorothy were married in London in 1920. They had four children—a son and three daughters. The son, Maurice, is Conservative M.P. for Farnham. The daughters married and there are a number of grandchildren.

The Queen sent a personal message of sympathy last night to Mr Macmillan.

Rebel Shells Near U.S. Air Base

THE United States Air Force yesterday began evacuating jet fighter bombers from the giant air base at Da Nang, South Vietnam.

Rebel shellfire had burst close to grounded aircraft and sleeping U.S. servicemen.

Ten U.S. Marines and airmen were wounded by shells.

Minutes after the shells landed a general evacuation order was issued. Jets roared into the sky.

Over 100 U.S. planes are believed based at this vital airfield, defended by 20,000 Marines.

Pagoda Captured.

Yesterday militant Buddhist monks backing the rebels warned the base would be wrecked unless U.S. Marines helped to force besieging Government troops of Premier Nguyen Cao Ky to withdraw from Da Nang.

In a bitter four-hour siege, Government tanks and troops captured the smallest of three pagodas held by rebellious local soldiers and Buddhist monks. Government planes strafed the area.

In Washington, President Johnson said he was watching the Vietnam situation very closely. He regretted diversions from the effort against the ...

The moment before the end—C...

MYSTE... HARBO...

A MOTORIST dashed ac... clothed into Broughty Fe... a young girl from drowning.

Then he drove off soaking giving his name.

The girl who owes her life to her unknown rescuer is 10-year-old Rhona Grant, 54 North Bank Street, Monifieth.

Rhona was returning from play at Castle Green with her cousin, David Grant (8), to her grandmother's house in Fisher Street when the accident happened.

She apparently lost her footing at the edge of the harbour and plunged over the side into 12 feet of water.

The rescuer was sitting in his car parked near the spot and, without wasting a second, he raced across the road and plunged in.

Rhona was unconscious... brought h...

COMMOTION

Rhona's father, motor mechanic Mr James Grant (41), was on his way to collect Rhona and her brother and take them home when he saw the commotion and ... that his daughter ...

... contractor Mr Harry Lawson's office nearby and Mr Lawson phoned an ambulance.

husband —" the hospital with her told us there is no doubt that this man saved Rhona's life.

"I don't know how we can thank him enough."

Rhona was detained in the Royal Infirmary for observation.

CRASH LANDIN...

What's the best way to bring up a boy to make a man of him?

See Page 11

MAY 22, 1966

Henry Cooper's valiant attempt to win the world heavyweight title failed again in this rematch with Cassius Clay as he was then known.

The following page carries the television schedules for Christmas Day nineteen sixty six.

Included on the page are a couple of advertisements with a festive theme.

26   The Sunday Post, December 25, 1966.

TELEVISION AND RADIO

B.B.C. 1 TV

9.30—WELCOME CHRISTMAS.
10.10—MAK THE SHEEP STEALER.
11.0—SING IN EXULTATION.
12.0 — LESLIE CROWTHER meets the kids.
12.44—WEATHER.
12.45—THE LUCY SHOW.
1.10—THE ANDY WILLIAMS SHOW.
2.0—THE ROYAL PALACES OF BRITAIN.
3.0—QUEEN'S MESSAGE.
3.5—BILLY SMART'S CIRCUS.
4.0—DISNEY TIME.
4.40—ALADDIN. with Arthur Askey.
6.5—NEWS AND WEATHER.
6.10—WAR ON WANT.
6.15—THE TWO HILLS.
6.45—CHRISTMAS CAROLS.
7.25 — THE BLACK AND WHITE MINSTREL SHOW.
8.0—THE KEN DODD SHOW, starring the Bachelors.
8.45—THE COMANCHEROS, with John Wayne.
10.25—NEWS AND WEATHER.
10.30—DR FINLAY'S CASE BOOK.
11.20—WEATHER.
11.22 — THE CHRISTMAS STORY.
11.52—KIRK NEWS POSTSCRIPT.

ULSTER TV

As STV, except for:—
10.20—A TOUR OF CAROLS.
1.10—TALES FROM DICKENS.
2.1—CLIFF RICHARD AND THE SHADOWS.
3.7—FEATURE FILM. " Sabrina Fair."
5.5—SNOW WHITE.
6.15—LOVE CAME DOWN AT CHRISTMAS.
8.55—FILM. " Strange Lady in Town."
11.55 — THIS CHRISTMAS NIGHT, with Rev. W. B. Neill, B.A., senior curate of St Elizabeth's Dundonald.

STV

9.40 — A CHRISTMAS MESSAGE.
9.50—A MERRY CHRISTMAS.
10.20—A TOUR OF CAROLS.
11.0 — M A N C H E S T E R CATHEDRAL.
12.10—THE ROYAL PALACES.
1.10—GALA OPPORTUNITY KNOCKS.
2.0—CLIFF RICHARD AND THE SHADOWS in " Wish Upon a Wishbone."
3.0—THE QUEEN'S MESSAGE.
3.5—MICHAEL SHAYNE.
4.0—POLICE CALL.
4.10—BATMAN.
4.35 — CHRISTMAS CAVALCADE.
6.0—NEWS.
6.15—WEATHERWISE.
6.35—THE HAPPY BIRTHDAY.
7.25 — SECOMBE, FRIENDS, AND RELATIONS.
8.55—THE BIG SHOW presents "The Big Knife."
10.15—NEWS.
10.25—THE BIG SHOW (part 2).
11.5—T H E E A M O N N ANDREWS SHOW.
11.55—LATE CALL.

BORDER TV

As STV, except for:—
10.10 — A CHRISTMAS MESSAGE. Rt. Rev. Leonard Small, O.B.E., D.D., Moderator of the General Assembly of the Church of Scotland.
1.10—TALES FROM DICKENS.
3.0—THE QUEEN'S MESSAGE TO THE COMMONWEALTH.
3.7—FEATURE FILM. " Rio Bravo."
5.30 — BATMAN (part 2). " Walk the Straight and Narrow."
8.55—EMERGENCY WARD 10.
9.50 — FEATURE FILM. " The Flying Scot " (part 1).
10.25—THE FLYING SCOT. Part 2.
11.55 — CHRISTMAS DAY EPILOGUE.
12.0—GOODNIGHT.

B.B.C. 2 TV

3.0—THE QUEEN.
3.5 — THE WORLD OF JACQUES-YVES COSTEAU.
4.0—OH, MR PORTER.
5.20 — THE LENINGRAD STATE KIROV BALLET.
6.10—NEWSYEAR '66.
7.25—HORIZON CHRISTMAS SPECIAL.
8.0—DIE FLEDERMAUS.
10.10—MEET THE SWINGLES.
10.30—LATE NIGHT LINE-UP.
11.30 — MONSIEUR BEAUCAIRE.

GRAMPIAN TV

As STV, except for:—
3.7—FEATURE FILM. " Great Expectations."
3.20—BARBARINA.
5.25—CARTOON TIME.
8.55—FILM PREMIERE.
10.25—FILM PREMIERE. Part 2.
11.55—EVENING PRAYERS.
12.0—WEATHER.

★ RADIO ★

HOME (371 m.).
7.50 — Sunday Reading. 8.0—News. 8.10 — The Babe of Bethlehem. 8.50 — Christmas Day Parade. 9.0—News. 9.5—Christmas Morning Service. 10.30 — Where the Tribes Go Up. 11.0—Scarlatti and Schubert. 11.15—Pick of the Week. 12.15—Welcome Yule. 1.0—The Queen; News. 1.10 — Any Questions? 2.0 — Christmas Party. 2.30 — The Sunday Play. 4.0—Happy the Man. 4.45—The Old Old Story. 5.15—Down Your Way. 6.0 — News. 6.10 — Letter from America. 6.25 — Week's Good Cause. 6.30—Grand Hotel. 7.15—Scottish Life and Letters. 8.0—Evening Service. 8.30—Hard Times (part 4). 9.0—Your Hundred Best Tunes. 10.0 — News. 10.10—Edwardian Gems of the Music-Hall. 10.50—The Epilogue. 11.0—News. 11.2—Music on Christmas Night.

LIGHT (247 m.; 1500 m.).
8.55 — The First Day of the Week. 7.0 — News. 9.0 — Family Choice. 9.30—The Queen. 9.35—Family Choice. 10.0 — Mrs Mills' Christmas Party. 10.31—Easy Beat. 11.30 — People's Service. 11.55—Good Listening. 12.0 — Five-Way Family Favourites. 1.30—The Billy Cotton Band Show. 2.15 — Tom Jones Sings. 3.0 — Semprini Serenade. 4.0 — The Dee-Jays of Christmas. 5.0 — Christmas Carols. 6.0—Round the Horne. 6.30—Sing Something Simple. 6.55—Wireless for the Blind Appeal. 7.0 — The Clithroe Kid. 7.30—News. 7.35—Bing Crosby. 8.30—Sunday Half-Hour. 9.0—Movie-Go-Round. 9.30—The Men from the Ministry. 10.0—Records for You. 12.0—The Jazz Scene. 2.0—News.

THIRD (464 m.; 194 m.).
8.0—News. 8.5—What's New? 9.0—News. 9.4—Christmas Music. 9.30 — The Queen. 9.35 — Your Christmas Choice. 11.0 — Music Magazine. 12.0—From the Salzburg Festival. 12.56—Talking About Music. 1.30—From the Salzburg Festival. 2.5—Haydn. 3.12—Tosca. 3.38—Chopin. Tosca. 5.0 — Music Quiz. 5.40—Schutz. 6.35 — Choices. 7.10—Beethoven and Schumann. 8.5—The Story of Jorkel Hayforks. 8.25 —Beethoven and Schumann. 9.10—The Hare. 10.15—Stravinsky. 11.0—News.

RADIO SCOTLAND (242 m.).
8.0 — Breakfast Beat. 10.0—Herald of Truth. 10.30—Stateside 50. 12.30 — Sweet Music. 1.45—Good Neighbours. 1.45—Ready, Youth. 2.0 — Knock About Pop. 2.30 — 1/2. 5.0 — Back Track. 7.0—The World Tomorrow. 7.30—McLaughlin's Ceilidh. 8.0—Open Door. 8.30 — Sweet and Low. 9.30 —Radio Bible Class. 10.0 — Sweet and Low. 11.0—Swing Shift.

LUXEMBOURG (208 m.).
6.0—Don Wardell. 8.0—Tony's 208 Party. 8.45—A Christmas Card from Mecca. 9.0—Tony and Don's Christmas Requests. 9.45—Ready, Steady, Radio! 10.0—Don Wardell. 10.30—Ready, Steady, Radio! 10.45 — Curry's Corner. 11.0 — Top Twenty. 12.0 — Midnight with Matthew. 12.30—Music in the Night.

The Sunday Post 16th January 1966

OOR WULLIE 70 Years Young

The Sunday Post 1st May 1966

The Sunday Post 11th September 1966

OOR WULLIE 70 Years Young

The Sunday Post 24th September 1967

OOR WULLIE 70 Years Young

The Sunday Post 8th October 1967

The Sunday Post 21st January 1968

OOR WULLIE 70 Years Young

The Sunday Post 12th May 1968

The Sunday Post 28th January 1968

OOR WULLIE 70 Years Young

The Sunday Post 9th March 1969

1976

The Sunday Post, July 4, 1976.

The Sunday Post

PRINTED AND PUBLISHED EVERY SUNDAY MORNING.

No. 3697.

[REGISTERED AT THE POST OFFICE AS A NEWSPAPER.]

SUNDAY, JULY 4, 1976.

Morning Special

TV and Radio — Page 17.

Price 8p.

There's A Long, Long Trail A-Winding...

HEATWAVE SWIMMERS DROWN

What Happened To The New Rescue Craft?

AFTER an escape from drowning at Balmedie Beach, north of Aberdeen, questions were being asked about a rescue craft, provided for the first time only three days ago.

But yesterday it failed to operate.

A Grampian Regional spokesman said a full investigation would be carried out as to why the craft was not available.

The vessel was provided at a cost of £1200 as part of an overall development in the recreational facilities at Balmedie, which in recent years has become popular with swimmers and sunseekers.

Yesterday Roger Hales, of Aberdeen, was swimming 150 yards offshore when he got into difficulties.

Heart Massage

Four lifeguards on duty at the beach as part of the new safety measures, swam out and brought him ashore.

They tried to revive him while still in the water. Heart massage was continued on the beach.

Mr Hales was taken by ambulance to Aberdeen Royal Infirmary. A late report last night from Foresterhill stated his condition was still serious.

Mr Hales (29), a salesman, of 1 Princes Crescent, Dyce, was bathing with his wife Rosemary (25) when he got into difficulties.

She went to his rescue but also found herself in trouble. Their plight was spotted by the beach patrol.

Mrs Hales, after being assisted ashore by friends, was taken to the outpatient department at Woolmanhill, Aberdeen, but was later released.

AS the heatwave continued this week-end, three men died in separate drowning accidents.

Two of the tragedies occurred when men went swimming with friends.

The third involved a 63-year-old man who drowned in the Monkland Canal in the Milton district of Glasgow.

His body was discovered in the middle of the canal by two schoolboys, who searched the area when they found clothing lying on the bank.

He has not yet been identified.

In accident No. 2, a 31-year-old man drowned when he went for a swim near Lochearnhead late on Friday night during a fishing trip.

Two friends tried to find him, but they ran into difficulties and had to swim ashore.

Police from Perth were still searching for the man's body yesterday.

The third tragedy happened at a reservoir in Bathgate. William Agnew (36), 58 Glenmavis Drive, Bathgate, had gone for a swim with friends.

Ronald McBridge (26), of Bathgate, told "The Sunday Post," "I saw Willie's head above the water, then turned away. When I looked back he was gone.

"We thought nothing about it at the time. We reckoned Willie had gone home."

Today's Weather

SUNNY periods, coastal fog patches. Wind south-easterly, light or moderate. Hot inland, max. 24 to 25C (75 to 77F), but cooler on coasts.

New Rover For Mark An

PRINCESS ANNE and Captain Mark Phillips

AS the heatwave sizzled on, there were strained tempers yesterday on the A74, Scotland's main road to the South.

Over 3000 cars an hour were passing through Carlisle compared with a normal average of 500.

But for those holidaymakers hoping for a quick getaway, there was a nine-mile-long disappointment.

That's how big the jam was between Abington and Crawford.

As the afternoon wore on and the temperature built up, so did the congestion.

Much of the traffic was from Clydebank and Greenock as local holiday fortnights got under way.

To add to the problem, road works reduced some parts of the A74 to single lane.

A.A. patrols were swamped with breakdown calls. By mid-afternoon, motorists faced a three-hour wait for attention.

Main problem was overheating.

● The R.A.C. yesterday ticked-off motorists using a dangerous method of preventing their cars overheating.

A spokesman said some cars were being driven with bonnet lids slightly raised.

"This is highly dangerous, as the air pressure under the bonnet when the car is moving can cause it to fly open suddenly."

● Firemen from four stations were last night battling to contain an extensive outbreak in woodlands between Grange and Keith.

The blaze, which spread rapidly through the tinder-dry forest, began in the late afternoon at Balloch Hill, part of the large pine forest between Huntly and Keith.

It was tackled by units from Dufftown, Aberlour, Rothes and Huntly.

Yesterday, Mr Arthur Cuthbert, the Forestry Commission district officer for Aberdeenshire and Banffshire, stressed the forests in the North-East were at great risk from people throwing lit cigarettes from car windows.

Ulster Baby Bor

Seven Trapped After Perthshire Accident

SEVEN people were trapped yesterday when two cars were in collision at Collace crossroads, near Kinrossie.

Four were freed before the arrival of the emergency tender from Perth Fire Brigade.

Firemen released the remaining three.

Five were taken by ambulance to Perth Royal Infirmary and later four were transferred to Bridge of Earn Hospital.

...leading specialists on gunshot wounds, a bullet was found lodged in her side.

Five people were killed in Ulster shootings yesterday.

A Scottish soldier died after being shot in the head by a sniper at a pedestrian checkpoint in Londonderry.

He was Gunner William Miller (19), of Larkhall, Lanarkshire.

He was single and only arrived in the city on Tuesday.

...by one of the ...Bar, ...similar incident in ...Friday.

The Irish Republic didn't escape trouble.

A series of bomb blasts hit four top hotels last night in a carefully co-ordinated operation.

One bomb was at the famous Gresham Hotel, Dublin.

At the Royal George Hotel, Limerick, an eight-year-old boy and wedding guests suffered shock and abrasions.

But, at the Great Southern Hotel in Rosslare and Ki...

JULY 4, 1976

The long hot summer of seventy six saw massive traffic jams as people fled the cities, for the cooler coasts, and forest fires raged. It wasn't all bad news, however, as foreign tourists flocked to Scotland to enjoy the benefits of the weak pound.

114

As Foreign Visitors Arrive In Their Thousands

They're All Raving About Scotland

HOW do foreign visitors see Scotland these days, as we struggle on through the economic crisis?

Our overseas image may not be so hot, but one benefit of the falling pound is tourists have been flocking here in droves.

What do they think of us? What surprises them most about Scotland? "Sunday Post" reporters put these questions to tourists up and down the country last week. Here's what they had to say—

★ I'm surprised at how hard working the Scots are. We hear so many conflicting stories back home. It's obvious to visitors most people are working harder to get things right. I do wish you'd look happier. You've so much to enjoy in this country. — Laureen Bowman (housewife), Minnesota, U.S.A.

★ Your prices are a revelation. I've just paid £10 for a pair of shoes that would have cost me double back home. — Roger Hogben (56), Adelaide, Australia.

★ I never realised Scottish people were so polite. Wherever you go, people are always mannerly. You seem to take the politeness on to the roads as well. The standard of driving is far superior to that of Greece. — Stavros Stambolidis, Athens.

★ It's simply surprising that everything is so normal. I'd read that Britain was so hard up we should be thinking of sending you food parcels. It seems to me Scotland will survive the financial crisis better than most. But cheer up. Why do you all look so glum? — Jean Armitage, Edmonton, Canada.

★ Scottish people don't seem to show any urgency, yet things get done all the same. They've plenty of time for visitors. We were in a shop in Aberdeen buying gifts. After we'd left, the lady ran after us because we'd given her too much money. — Jorgen Kessler, Darmstadt, W. Germany.

★ Scots take more time about the way they live. They're less worried and anxious than in France. — Mrs Francoise Thiebeaux (27), Rheims.

Smuggle It!

★ The water amazes me. The way you waste it seems terrible at first, till you realise there's so much of it. Maybe Scotland should start selling water instead of oil. It tastes so good I'm thinking of smuggling some home! — Miss Cathy Peterson, Christchurch, New Zealand.

★ I expected to find everyone anxious about the state of the country. Instead, I see smiling faces, prosperous-looking people, shops filled with goods. Many things are only one third the price they would pay in Sweden. — Olof Hellgren, Bjorka Eskjo, Sweden.

★ Scots strike me as honest and fair. Shopkeepers think nothing of telling you where you can buy goods cheaper than they're selling them. That's astonishing! — Genny Simson (schoolteacher), Sheperton, Nr. Melbourne.

★ I thought you were on the verge of economic disaster. I was prepared to find all kinds of shortages and soaring prices. But shops are crammed with luxury goods at unbelievably low prices. People certainly aren't going hungry. With your prices, I can see Scotland becoming the top tourist spot in Europe. — Lindsay Campbell (28), Auckland, New Zealand.

★ I'm surprised at the number of down-and-outs in Glasgow. I didn't think you had problems like this because of your government's welfare services. — Mark Sterling, New York.

So Friendly

★ I'd expected Scots to be difficult to talk to. It just isn't the case. The reputation you have abroad is totally different from the facts. I love Scotland, simply because of the people. — Miss Dora Val, Venice.

★ I'm surprised there are so few private cars. Still, you have very efficient public transport. — Sidney Futterman, Long Island, New York.

★ I expected to find austerity, with goods scarce and people tightening their belts. I'm stunned at the high standard of living! Your roads are crowded with shiny new cars. There's no evidence you're worried about economic plight. I don't know how it's done. — Stanford Terhune (35), Massachusetts.

★ There were stories in the American Press about how bad things were here. I think that was because the Government wanted to discourage Americans from taking their dollars out of the country. We like it, now we're here. We've been impressed most of all by your public transport. The buses are clean and convenient, and the fares low. — Kenneth E. Wilson (73), Oregon, U.S.A.

★ I thought Scotland would be much wilder and more barren. I'm surprised it's so green and fertile. I expected a rather gloomy land. Instead I find a warm, friendly attractive country. — Mrs Patricia Raconni (28), Milan.

★ I'd heard Glasgow was a dirty industrial city, to be avoided. I'm going to stay longer in Glasgow than I planned. It's a lovely city. You've so many parks to walk in, so many shopping areas where you can walk free from traffic and there are flowers everywhere. It's one of the nicest cities I've visited on my European tour. — Anne Vaateri (student), Finland.

★ I'm surprised how "uncommercial" the Highlands are. If we had Loch Ness back home, you wouldn't get near it for hotels, shopping centres, souvenir shops, restaurants. You may be losing some money on the deal, but it's refreshing. — Al Rushton (electrician), California.

★ Big Scottish breakfasts are wonderful. And my husband says your beer is better and colder than English beer! — Mrs Henny Hogerwert (49), Rotterdam.

Your Star Story Can Win £50

EACH week "The Sunday Post" will consider any story originating from a reader for an award in the following star categories —

★ ★ ★ ★ ★ — £50
★ ★ ★ ★ — £40
★ ★ ★ — £30
★ ★ — £20
★ — £10

All you have to do is give us brief details. The story may be aimed at any of our pages, from news and features to sport. It can be on any subject under the sun.

At least one star prize will be paid each week at the Editor's discretion. Any Readers' Letters will automatically be considered. Otherwise, stories should be addressed to — "Star Story," The Sunday Post, 144 Port Dundas Road, Glasgow G4 0HZ.

Or you may phone any of our offices with a story and ask that it be considered for a "Star Story" prize.

Not all categories of prizes need be awarded each week.

But all stories will also be considered for publication at our normal rates.

The Editor's decision is final.

Tom Lavery had a ten year spell as Broons artist.
The Sunday Post 27th October 1974

OOR WULLIE 70 Years Young

The Sunday Post 6th August 1978

The Sunday Post 7th January 1979

OOR WULLIE 70 Years Young

Bob Nixon, one of Britain's favourite comic illustrators helped out in the early 90's.
The Sunday Post 29th July 1990

THE BROONS 70 Years Young

Peter Davidson, the current artist, illustrated the Broons in his first spell in the eighties.

The Sunday Post 10th January 1982

Ken H. Harrison took on the illustrating duties for the greater part of the nineties.
The Sunday Post 28th October 1990

The Sunday Post 20th June 1982

The Sunday Post

No. 4209   Price 26p

MAY 25, 1986.

SCOTLAND'S TOP-SELLING SUNDAY NEWSPAPER

Morning Special

Sunday Post Random Tests Reveal 'Chernobyl Cocktail' Still In Scotland

RADIATION—IS IT REALLY ALL OVER?

THIS week The Sunday Post has set out to make some sense of the confusion in the aftermath of the Chernobyl nuclear disaster because people are still very concerned at conflicting evidence.

Questions being asked are—Just how much radiation has affected the country? Are Government figures giving the whole story? Has it all blown over with the cloud?

We sought the help of an independent scientific body, The Natural Environment Research Council.

With one of their scientists, Roger Cummins, from the Institute of Terrestrial Ecology, at Banchory, a Sunday Post man drove the length of the country from Aberdeenshire, taking geiger counter readings, vegetation samples and measuring the radiation in the atmosphere at selected sites.

The samples will be analysed in full at the Institute's Merlewood Centre, Grange-over-Sands, Cumbria.

The complex tests mean the full results can't be published until next week.

So far official radiation figures released by the National Radiological Protec-

tion Board have been based on the amount of radioactive iodine deposited.

It's the substance which has prompted speculation that drinking contaminated milk could cause cancer.

Official sources have stressed the ... on the ground dis... has a half ... which mea... harmful ra... per cent e...

Nasty

Howev... tially lon... another ... fallout—... tope, Ca... danger... a half ...

In ... around ... This ... rand...

W...

Family's holiday ... Balmoral Castle.

Then south through the farmlands of Perthshire into the major population centres of Scotland and finally north-west England where some of the highest radiation readings in the country are being found.

One independent expert, Peter Taylor of the Political Ecology Research Group, Oxford ... says that Caesium 137 ... harmful

THE FIELD READINGS

Balmoral	7
Spittal of Glenshee	9
Blairgowrie	5
New Scone	12
Dunblane	15
Coatbridge	7
Lesmahagow	13
Abington	5
Beattock	7
Lockerbie	6
Carlisle	5

plutonium emission... can the geiger counter tell how harmful the radiation is, because it cannot identify the particular element giving it out.

Only laboratory analysis of our samples will reveal the exact levels of fallout.

Dr Francis Livens, head of the ITE lab which will carry out the analysis, says there's no great gap between the results at the various sites.

The "Chernobyl Cocktail" is a particular mix of elements which scientists can quickly identify.

Where Caesium 137 is found, it can only be as a result of the Chernobyl cloud. It doesn't occur naturally in the environment.

• Words of encouragement for Omar Khalifa from the Prince and Princess of Wales.

THE Prince and Princess of Wales held aloft the Sports Aid torch of hope yesterday as a gesture of support for the famine relief campaign they have enthusiastically backed.

The torch, lit from the embers of a camp fire in Sudan, was delivered to Buckingham Palace by Sports Aid athlete Omar Khalifa.

His date with the Royal couple came during another exhausting day for the 29-year-old Sudanese athlete which saw him running in Dublin, jetting into Heathrow to be greeted by Mrs Thatcher, and going on to London for a visit to Lambeth Palace and another long run.

Then it was back to the airport for a Concorde flight to New York.

Last year the Prince and Princess joined Band Aid mastermind Bob Geldof at the highly successful Live Aid concert at Wembley.

But a tired Geldof backed out of his visit to New York at the last minute last night, announcing he'd take part in the run in London instead.

The Sports Aid founder was due to start today's big race outside the United Nations building in New York, but a week-long dose of acute tonsilitis took its toll and doctors told him not to make the journey.

THE New York race will be one of 266 simultaneous races in cities in 75 countries around the world. The fund-raising runs will involve up to 20 million people.

In Scotland, 80,000 are expected to take part, including 15,000 keep-fit enthusiasts who will take part in a mass work-out at the Scottish Exhibition Centre in Glasgow. Each has paid £5 towards the fund.

For those who do not participate in the runs but would like to make a cash donation, 500 volunteers are manning telephone lines throughout the UK this weekend to take credit card pledges. The Telethon has already raised over £60,000.

The numbers are London (01) 636 1566, Birmingham (021) 780 4122, Belfast (0232) 232 668 and Glasgow (041) 357 1774.

• For local events, see Page 4.

20 INJURED IN DUNDEE MINI BUS HORROR
SEE PAGE 2

• Roger Cummins of the Institute of Terrestrial Ecology takes his readings at a site near Coatbridge.

MAY 25, 1986

The fallout from Chernobyl nuclear plant was causing concern in 1986, with radiation levels being monitored. On the back page the Mexico World Cup dominated the headlines, while domestically Graeme Souness was making news.

1986

The Sunday Post, June 8, 1986.

STOP PRESS

STOP PRESS

LEAVING LIVERPOOL
Ian Rush has decided to join Italian giants Juventus for £3 million. He will fly to Italy tonight to complete the deal which makes him most expensive British player.

Doug Baillie's WORLD CUP FILE
MEXICO 86

TOP-SECRET SCOTS

FRANZ BECKENBAUER is scoffing at the veil of secrecy Alex Ferguson has thrown round his team selection for today's make-or-break World Cup tie.

The Scotland boss banned TV cameras, radio and Press from the squad's last training session in the stadium before kick-off.

By contrast the West German coach told me, "Nothing the Scots can do can surprise us. I know they are well organised, but it doesn't matter what system or players they use. We will be ready for them.

"We know their players, their style and how they will approach the match."

Confident words indeed from The Kaiser as he spoke at his luxurious training HQ 25 miles outside Mexico City. And I have to report there is an alarming air of confidence about the whole place.

If the Germans are worried about anything Fergie might have up his sleeve, they are doing a grand job of hiding it.

Franz, however, did admit he expects Scotland to play better against his team than against the Danes.

"They will put more into the game because they have to get a good result to stay in the competition," he added.

"The Scots will play with their hearts, but we are strong enough to beat them no matter how late Alex. Ferguson holds up his selection.

"My team will be the same as started against Uruguay—with one exception. Pierre Littbarski will take over from Andreas Brehme in the midfield.

"Karl-Heinz Rummenigge is about 90% fit, but will only be used as a substitute."

COMPLETELY DIFFERENT

Fergie meantime is sticking to his guns—no team till 60 minutes before kick-off.

But don't be surprised if he comes up with something completely different this time. Indeed the Scottish boss has bet me 10 dollars I won't be able to name his team.

I won't even try, but I look for Steve Nicol dropping out to make way for Eamonn Bannon. There could also be a place for Stevie Archibald now that Charlie Nicholas has no chance of making it.

The Barcelona star, so near to selection against Denmark, could join forces up front with Paul Sturrock, who has made a miraculous recovery from the ankle injury picked up in the opening match.

All that's speculation though. The team manager remains tight-lipped on who will play.

"The players won't be told till nearer the kick-off," was how Fergie put it. "The team against Denmark was leaked. I don't want that to happen this time."

Who will win the battle between the confident Kaiser and the secretive Scot? I'd love to say the latter, but I feel it will be the former!

ROBSON GIVEN DEADLINE

BRYAN ROBSON has been given 48 hours to prove he can carry on in the World Cup.

The England captain, plagued by a shoulder problem, was thought to have seen his last Mexico action when led off against Morocco, but now manager Bobby Robson has left the door open for the midfield man to reappear against Poland on Wednesday.

"We'll see how he goes in training during the next couple of days," said Robson. "He has been doing press-ups and is keen to stay. He doesn't want to go home."

Yesterday Manchester United chairman Martin Edwards had contacted England's H.Q.

© D. C. Thomson & Co. Ltd. 1986. Print

ROBSON GIVEN FITNESS

in Monterrey demanding the immediate return of his club's captain for an operation.

Bryan insists he is ready to play his part against the Poles . . . if selected.

"Obviously the shoulder isn't right, but if the manager is prepared to take a risk I'll take the risk as well."

While he battles for full fitness, Robson has questioned the tactics employed by his manager in Mexico.

"I think it's all about the team pattern. We aren't quite sure how we are playing. We are getting disjointed and it's not looking very good."

BRAZIL defender Edson will be out for at least 12 days with a twisted ankle suffered against Algeria.

Spanish players jump on teammate BUTRAGENO after scoring in the first minute against the Irish.

MOVEMENT ON THE TRANSFER FRONT

Frankfurt Interest In Gough

CHARLIE THE GREAT

"**C**HARLIE NICHOLAS is as good a player as I've seen in a Scottish jersey." A mighty compliment, but even more so when it comes from the great Paul Breitner.

The former West German star, who won a World Cup medal in 1974, saw the Arsenal star in action against Denmark and couldn't hide his admiration.

"Charlie could be a great player anywhere he wanted to play," Paul told me. "I can see him being a star in places like Spain, Italy and even South America."

Breitner, an executive with a sportswear firm, is in Mexico to make sure the West German players display his wares to good effect!

EINTRACHT FRANKFURT are keen to sign one of Scotland's World Cup stars and the West German outfit are prepared to pay big money.

The man they are after is Dundee United defender Richard Gough, who has already been the subject of a £600,000-plus bid by Rangers.

The German outfit, however, know the Tannadice club have flatly refused to sell their best player to any Premier League side and are poised to move in.

They have already had Gough watched in Dundee United colours and were highly impressed with his performance against Denmark on Wednesday.

Should the deal go through, Richard would join forces with former Rangers' striker Davie Mitchell, who signed for Eintracht after two good performances for Australia in the World Cup qualifying ties against Scotland.

Gough, however, still has two years of his contract to run with United and boss Jim McLean is determined to hold on to him.

"I WANT WOODS"

GRAEME SOUNESS has confirmed he wants Norwich's England reserve goalkeeper Chris Woods for Rangers. The deal is expected to cost at least £500,000.

Woods (26) is regarded as the man most likely to become England's first-choice goalkeeper when Peter Shilton eventually stands down.

Speaking at the Scotland H.Q. in Mexico, Souness said, "I've never hidden my admiration for Peter Shilton, but I believe Chris will become England's No. 1 after the World Cup.

"He has the ability to become the best goalkeeper in Britain. I have already said money is no object in getting the best for Rangers, and this is the proof."

"To respect the wishes of England manager Bobby Robson so that none of his players should be subjected to transfer speculation in Mexico, no more discussions will take place until their return."

Norwich admit negotiat-

IRISH GO DOWN FIGHTING

● IN ON THE MEXICO ACTION ●

SPAIN 2, N. IRELAND 1
(Half-time 2-0).

Scorers: Spain—Butragueno (one min), Salinas (18); N. Ireland—Clarke (47).

A COMEDY of errors. That's how this Guadalajara clash will go down in the history books.

Two down early in the first half, thanks to a couple of alarming slips at the back, Northern Ireland were never really in a position to repeat that famous scoreline in Valencia four years ago.

The Irish were caught out by a sucker punch in the opening minute. Michel gathered in the middle of the park, looked up, and struck a precision ball into the heart of the penalty box to the feet of Butragueno.

The "Vulture" responded with a measured side-of-the-foot shot past Jennings.

Caught cold by the first No. 2 was a disaster for skipper Sammy McIlroy. Twice he attempted to clear his lines. Twice he played the ball to an opponent, and his second error teed up Salinas for a sparkling left-footer from 18 yards.

Outplayed for long periods, Billy Bingham's lads never gave up and were rewarded with one of the most bizarre goals of the tournament.

Zubizarreta raced off his line to clear a loose ball, but wildly sliced it to Galleco. Under no pressure at all, the defender's knock-back was all the keeper was well off the mark and Clarke nipped in to head the goal simply.

Against all the odds, the Irish were back in the game they really had to win.

With Stewart and Hamilton on for Penney and Worthington, tempers flared and Victor was cautioned for a challenge on playmaker McCreery.

Northern Ireland—Jennings, Nicholl, Donaghy, O'Neill, McDonald, McCreery, Stewart, McIlroy, Whiteside, Worthington (Hamilton), Clarke.

Spain—Zubizarreta, Tomas, Camacho, Victor, Goicoechea, Gallego (Calderol), Gordillo (Caldere), Michel, Francisco, Salinas (Senor), Butragueno.

Referee—H. Brummeier, Austria.

● After the game Spain's coach Miguel Munoz complained about the Irish tactics. "They found themselves behind and came out in the second half attacking with everything they had, including their elbows. They tried to intimidate our defenders."

GROUP B.

	P.	W.	D.	L.	F.	A.
Mexico	1	1	1	0	0	1
Paraguay	1		1	1	0	1
Belgium	1	1	1	0	1	1
Iraq	1	0	0	1	1	1

Remaining matches—Today—Iraq v. Belgium; Wednesday—Iraq v. Mexico; Paraguay v. Belgium.

Last-Minute Penalty Save

MEXICO 1, PARAGUAY 1
(Half-time—1-0).

Scorers: Mexico—Flores (3 min.); Paraguay—Romero (85).

A LAST-MINUTE penalty save by Fernandez denied Mexico their second Group B victory. He dived to his right to push Sanchez's kick against a post and away to safety.

Paraguay deserved their point after fighting back to level four minutes from time with a Romero header.

Mexico had gone ahead through Flores after only two minutes. English referee George Courtney whistled for 86 free kick, against the host country. He booked local hero Romero for "play acting in the Sanchez tackle.

The booking—the Mexicans second of the tournament—means he will miss the last group match against Iraq on Wednesday.

Four other players, two from each side, were also cautioned.

GROUP C.

	P.	W.	D.	L.	F.	A.
Brazil						
Spain	1	1	0	0	1	0
N. Ireland	2	0	1	1	1	2
Algeria	1	0	0	1	0	1

Remaining matches—Thursday—N. Ireland v. Brazil; Algeria v. Spain.

POLES BEAT THE TRAP

POLAND 1, PORTUGAL 0.
(Half-time 0-0). Scorer—Smolarek (69 mins).

AFTER a dismal first half, this Group F match sprang to life with Poland earning their victory with a Smolarek goal.

For once the Portuguese offside trap was caught out as a clean through to slip the ball under the keeper.

This goal doubled the tally for Poland in Group as a whole.

East-

The Sunday Post 20th October 1991

The Sunday Post 23rd May 1982

The Sunday Post 8th December 1991

The Sunday Post 4th September 1983

OOR WULLIE 70 Years Young

GETTIN' READY FOR CHRISTMAS

AH'M GETTING A'THING ORGANISED IN ADVANCE.

FIRST, I'LL HANG UP MY STOCKING.

AN' LEAVE OOT A GLASS O' MILK FOR SANTA AND A MINCE PIE FOR RUDOLPH.

I KEN FINE IT'S JUST PA THAT AYE EATS IT—BUT I DINNA WANT TO LET ON I KNEW ABOOT IT.

AH'M A SMART WRAPPER—AN' NO' THE SINGING KIND AFORE YE SAY IT!

NOW TAE PIT OOT MY PREZZIES TAE MA AN' PA UNDER THE TREE.

AN' SOMETHING FOR HARRY...I DINNA BOTHER WRAPPING IT NICELY...

WUFF?

...'COS HE AYE OPENS IT EARLY ANYWAY! HEH!

RRRIP!

ON WI' MA'S BEST TABLE CLOTH...

...AN' THE BEST KNIVES AN' FORKS.

IT WIDNAE BE CHRISTMAS WITHOOT THE CRACKERS!

I'VE SENT A' MY CHRISTMAS CARDS, TIDIED MY ROOM... AYE, THAT'S ABOUT IT.

I CAN GO TO BED NOW — I CAN HARDLY WAIT.

BUT IT'S ONLY THE 22ND, WULLIE— CHRISTMAS DAY ISNAE 'TIL WEDNESDAY!

SUN 22

I KEN THAT! IT'S JUST I CANNA TAK' ALL THE WAITING— AH'M STAYING IN BED FOR THREE DAYS. G'NIGHT.

WHIT A LADDIE.

CHRISTMAS MORN—

IT WIZ WORTH A' THE WAITING! MERRY CHRISTMAS, A'BODY!

KEN. H. HARRISON.

The Sunday Post 22nd December 1991

The Sunday Post 9th October 1983

No. 4712 —9

January 28, 1996

The SUNDAY POST

Price 55p

Second Chance Hotline could win you £50,000 *Page 23*

Meet Virginia Ironside, our new agony aunt *Page 37*

Ten holidays to be won — plus 2000 at half price *Page 28*

Lucky four share rollover jackpot

FOUR LUCKY punters have scooped more than £10 million each in the second-largest National Lottery jackpot.

Operators Camelot said last night the second double-rollover bonanza produced a total jackpot of £40,223,600.

It was not immediately known whether the four winners, each netting £10,055,900, were individuals or syndicates.

As double-rollover fever gripped ... for the second time in a ... hed out a ... into

£10 million each for winning tickets

...under and abbot of the Samye Ling ... in Eskdalemuir —

JANEARY 28, 1996

In this year big lottery wins were a feature of The Sunday Post's front pages. Winter held the country in its grip. A forgotten pile of railway posters had provided a charity with a different kind of windfall.

This has happened only ... in the Lottery's 63 weeks.

Sixty winners who guessed five of the Lottery numbers plus the bonus ball will pick up £83,960, while 1713 who picked five will net £1838.

Camelot estimates good causes will benefit by £34 million.

No qualms

The leader of Scotland's Buddhists buys two tickets every week and has no qualms about the morality of the National Lottery.

Dr Akong Tulku Rinpoche —

our Inter-Faith building on the Holy Isle."

So far Dr Rinpoche hasn't had a win. If he did, he says he would immediately donate it to the Samye Ling centre.

A spokesman for the Samye Ling said, "In the light of the Prince of Wales's statement, we are applying to the Millennium Fund for help with our Holy Island Project."

Meanwhile, the abbot is still keeping his fingers crossed.

■ A competitor charges through the snow on a two-husky sled.

Huskies at home in the snow

THE SIBERIAN weather gripping Scotland provided the perfect conditions for the British Husky Racing Championships in Aberfoyle yesterday.

Competitors from across the country converged on Loch Ard

Forest for the fifth event in the seven-race series, which climaxes in Nairn in February. The heats in Aberfoyle finish today.

Six, four and two-dog sleds raced through the snow-covered forest with teams of Siberian

Huskies and Alaskan Malamutes, reaching speeds of up to 20 mph.

Race organiser Ross Goldie believes the snowy conditions at Aberfoyle were perfect.

"Loch Ard Forest trail is ideal terrain for racing," she enthused.

National Lottery Winning Numbers ▶ (16) (17) (38) (41) (42) (43) **Bonus number** 28

1996

24   THE SUNDAY POST/ **March 17, 1996**

THE QUEEN OF SCOTS
PULLMAN—EACH WEEKDAY
KING'S CROSS **LONDON** and **GLASGOW** QUEEN STREET
LEEDS   HARROGATE   DARLINGTON   NEWCASTLE   EDINBURGH
BRITISH RAILWAYS

£600-700 ■ Having been stored under the bed, away from sunlight, the posters are in excellent condition.

THE NIGHT SCOTSMAN
Leaves King's Cross nightly at 10.25.

£10,000-15,000 ■ The pride of the collection. Back in the 1920s, the LNER began displaying their new poster designs annually in Edinburgh and London. They could be bought for just 5/- (25p)

She found £100,000 underneath the bed

A HOUSEWIFE struck gold when she was packing up her belongings to move house.

Under the bed in the spare room she was astonished to find more than 300 railway posters from the 1920s and '30s, all neatly rolled up and stacked away.

She was even more amazed when she was told by Onslow Auctions of London that they were worth around £100,000. The posters include scenes of

seaside resorts, trips to Scotland on the famous Flying Scotsman, industries, occupations, landmarks, historic buildings, towns and cities, spas, sleeping cars and restaurant services and travel to the continent.

Pride of place goes to *The Night Scotsman* painted by Alexeiff, a Russian artist best known for his work in film animation, who only did two posters.

It's expected to fetch £10,000 to £15,000. Others are estimated at £300 to £500 and a large number should fetch around £1000.

The woman, from East Anglia, has

her late husband to thank for her surprise haul.

As a boy, he'd been an avid train-spotter in London's East End and went on to serve an apprenticeship with London Underground.

While working for BR as an area maintenance manager in the late 50s, he salvaged the posters from Liverpool Street Station.

They were being thrown out with other advertising material.

Onslow's will put the collection under the hammer on Thursday. A major part of the proceeds will go to a children's charity.

£2500-3500 ■ Below — Scottish seaside resorts such as Cruden Bay feature in the collection.

GLEN OGLE
BRITISH RAILWAYS
PERTHSHIRE
SEE SCOTLAND BY RAIL

£200-300 ■ Picturesque Scottish scenes proved popular with rail passengers in the '20s and '30s

CRUDEN BAY

LNER

TAKE ME BY THE FLYING SCOTSMAN

OOR WULLIE 70 Years Young

The Sunday Post 15th December 1991

The Sunday Post 31st January 1993

OOR WULLIE 70 Years Young

The Sunday Post 7th May 1995

The Sunday Post 13th July 1997

The Sunday Post 18th June 1995

The Sunday Post 23rd September 1997

138

"A TIMELY

To celebrate the dawn of the new millennium, The Sunday Post requested special commemorative Broons and Oor Wullie strips to appear in The Sunday Post Magazine. It was a real bonanza week for fans as, besides the regular strips in the paper and these special strips in the supplement, there were also reprints of classic Dudley D. Watkins' strips, giving a triple dose of Broons and Oor Wullie.

CELEBRATION"

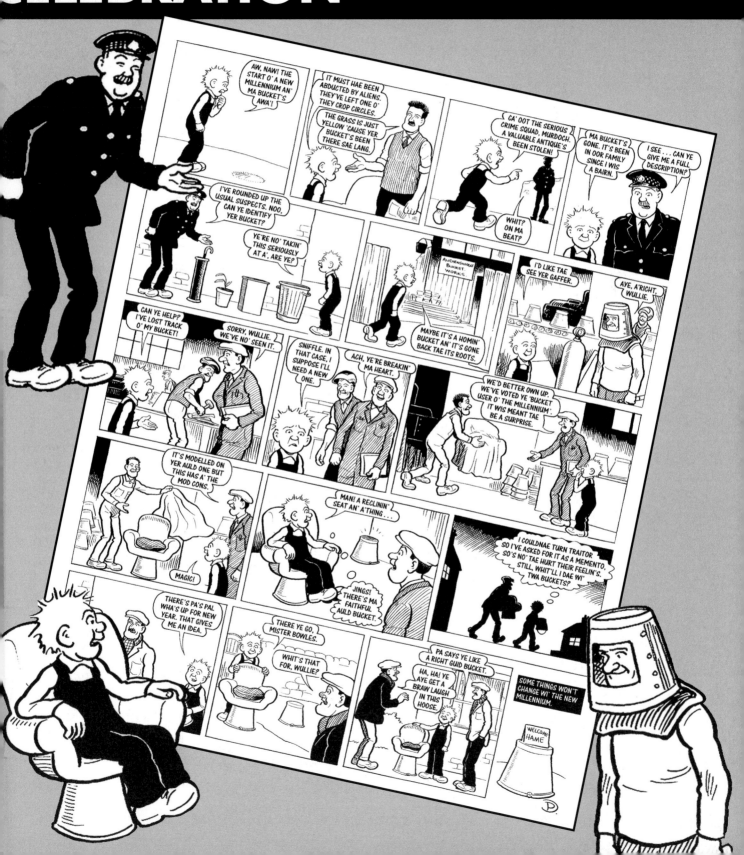

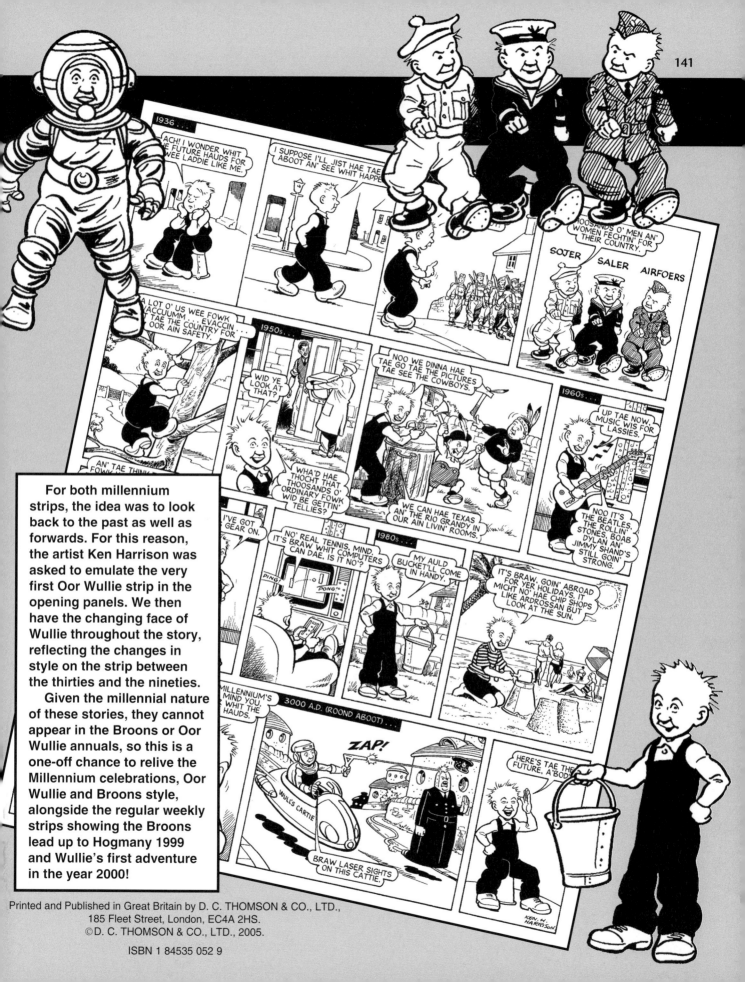

For both millennium strips, the idea was to look back to the past as well as forwards. For this reason, the artist Ken Harrison was asked to emulate the very first Oor Wullie strip in the opening panels. We then have the changing face of Wullie throughout the story, reflecting the changes in style on the strip between the thirties and the nineties.

Given the millennial nature of these stories, they cannot appear in the Broons or Oor Wullie annuals, so this is a one-off chance to relive the Millennium celebrations, Oor Wullie and Broons style, alongside the regular weekly strips showing the Broons lead up to Hogmany 1999 and Wullie's first adventure in the year 2000!

Printed and Published in Great Britain by D. C. THOMSON & CO., LTD.,
185 Fleet Street, London, EC4A 2HS.
©D. C. THOMSON & CO., LTD., 2005.

ISBN 1 84535 052 9